The House Full of Shoes

Written and Illustrated by

Kim Weinheimer

Published by
The Ja Company
Los Angeles, CA

Copyright © 2015 Kim Weinheimer
All rights reserved.

This book may not be reproduced, in whole or in part, stored in a retrieval system, or transmitted in any form or by any means — electronic, mechanical or other — without written permission from the publisher, except by a reviewer, who may quote brief passages in a review.

Published by
The Ja Company
9854 National Boulevard #483
Los Angeles, CA 90034

ISBN 978-1-4951-4254-3

Printed in the United States of America

Thank you to my family who made this book possible; Dorothy (mom), Melissa, Maria, Sarah and Kate – your support means everything.

Doreen, Jake (my son), and my husband Jake – I could not have done this without you.

It started in a small
and innocent way.

A baby was born,
it was his special day.

A new baby,
new booties to cover ten toes.

What started as a pair
would continue to grow.

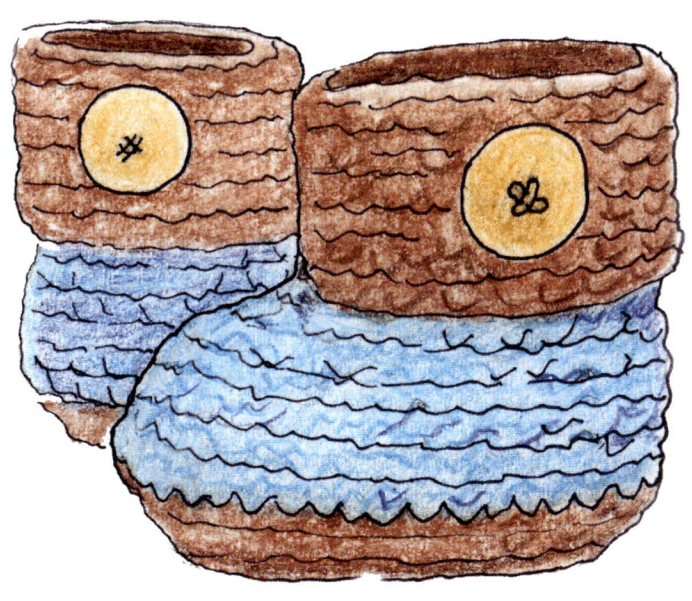

Booties and sockies
in all colors and shapes.

Some worn with horses,
some worn with capes.

Some worn for running.
Some worn for sun.

But clearly, so clearly,
all worn for fun.

As Mom picked up shoes,
pair after pair...

She had some good news
she wanted to share.

"You will soon have a brother!"
she said with a smile.

"It won't be too long,
I've known for a while."

And true to her word,
Bro soon came to be.

Family and friends
all came to see.

And of course they brought gifts.
That's what they do.

Cute little outfits,
each included shoes.

Now as the boys grew,
their shoes got too small...

But were quickly replaced
by a trip to the mall.

Shoes made for dress up.
Shoes just for play.

Shoes, shoes, shoes
and they got in the way.

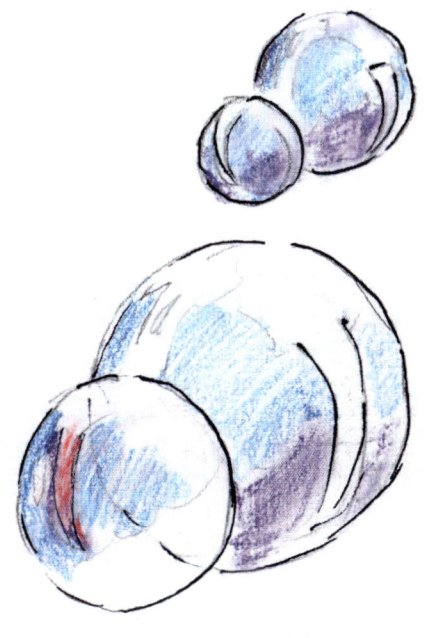

"Just pick up your shoes,
that's all that I ask."

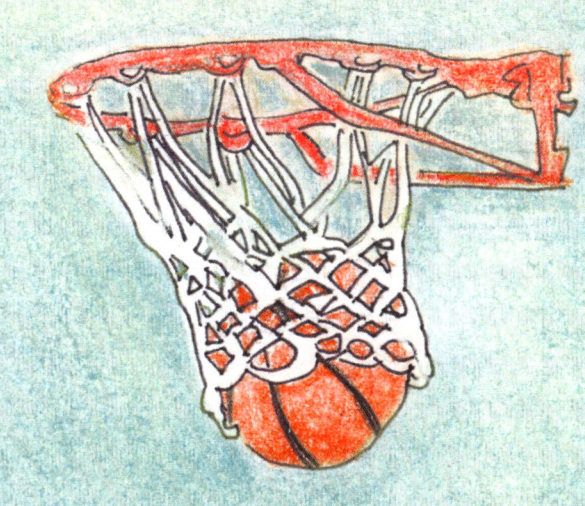

But there were games to be played and that was too large a task.

Now shoes tell a tale,
if you pay close attention.

They can speak volumes,
without even a mention.

Mom always knew
which friends came to call.

Seasons were told...

Spring,

Summer,

Winter...

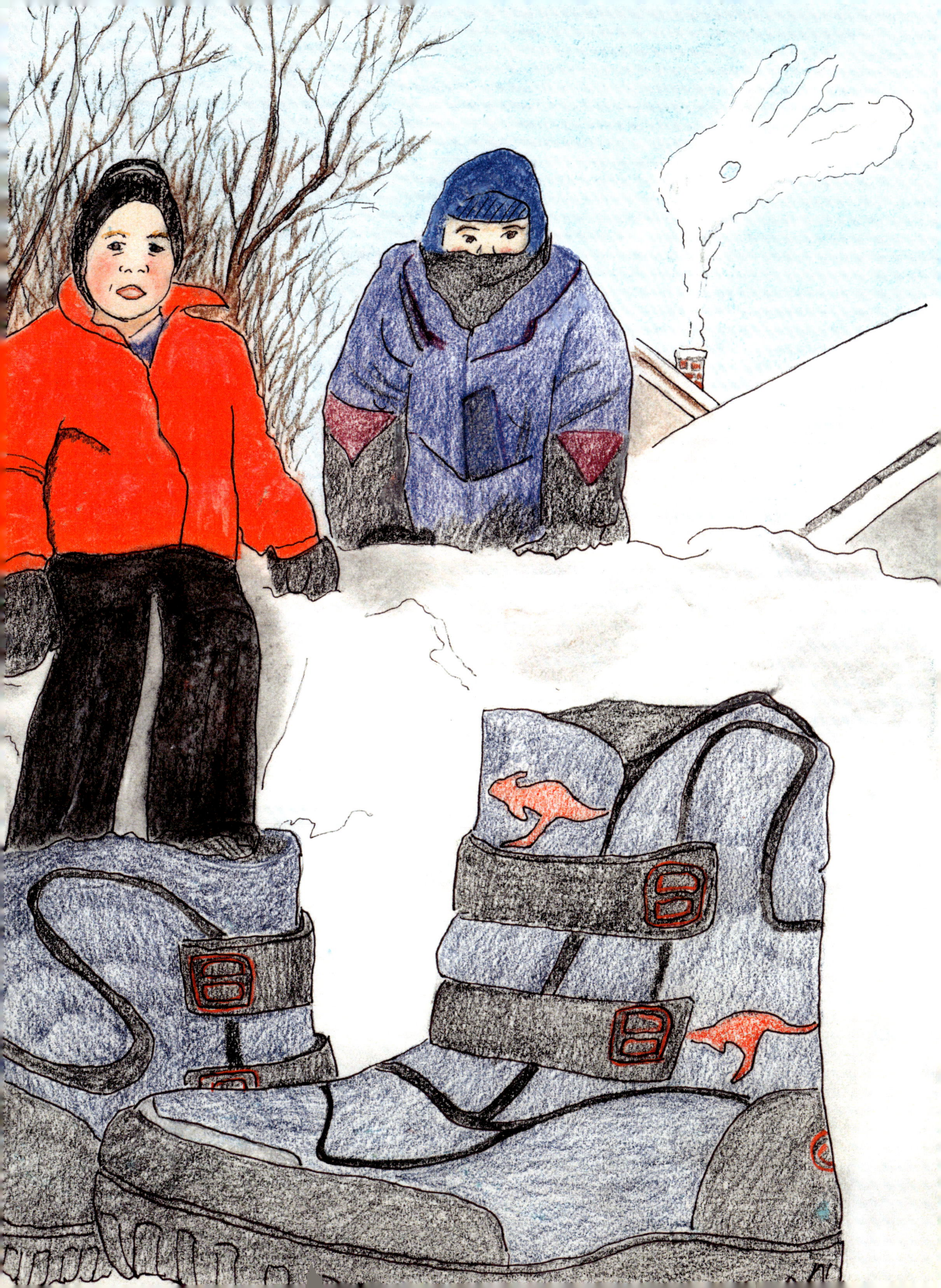

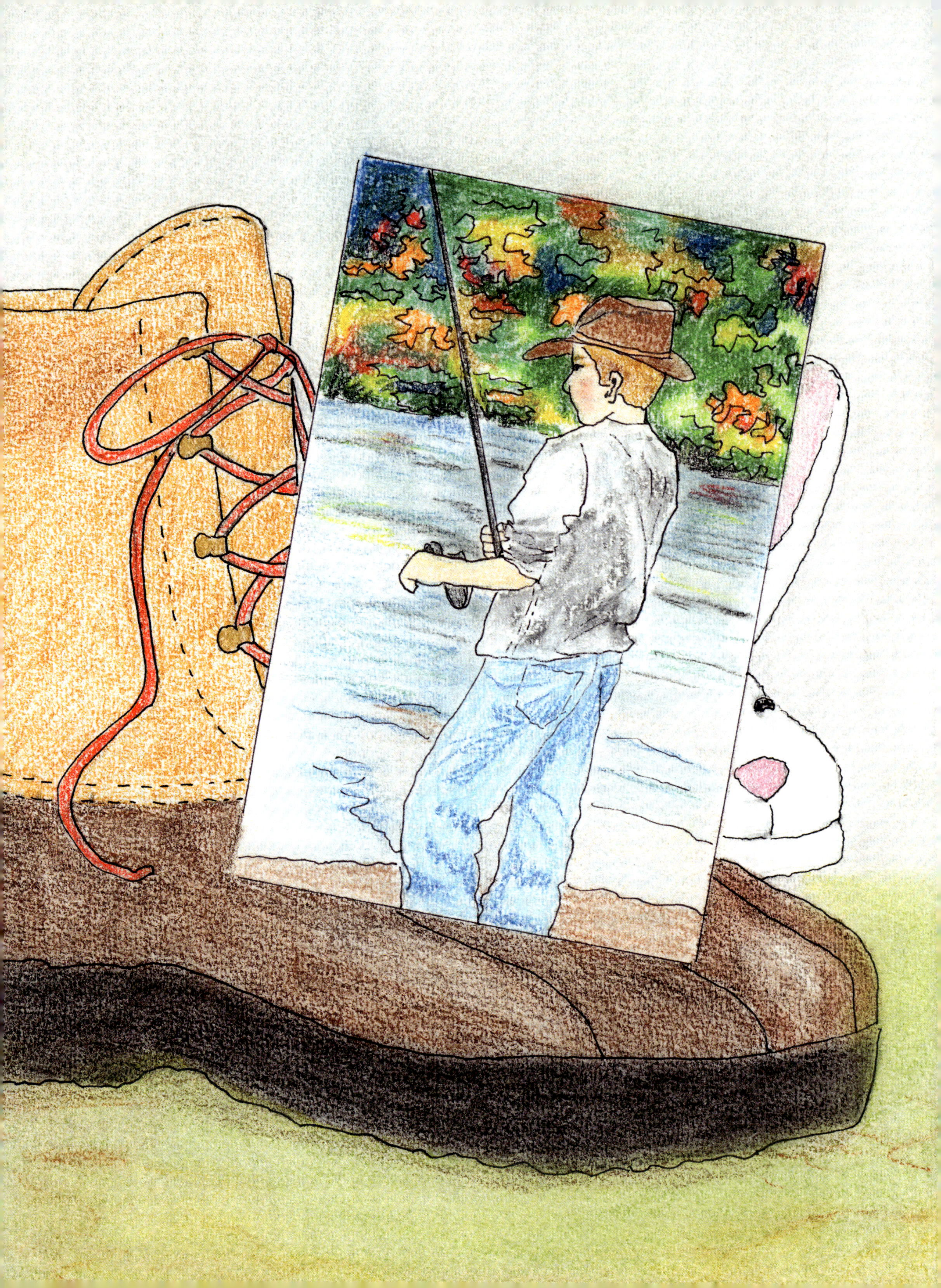

and Fall.

They told what the boys did while Mom was away.

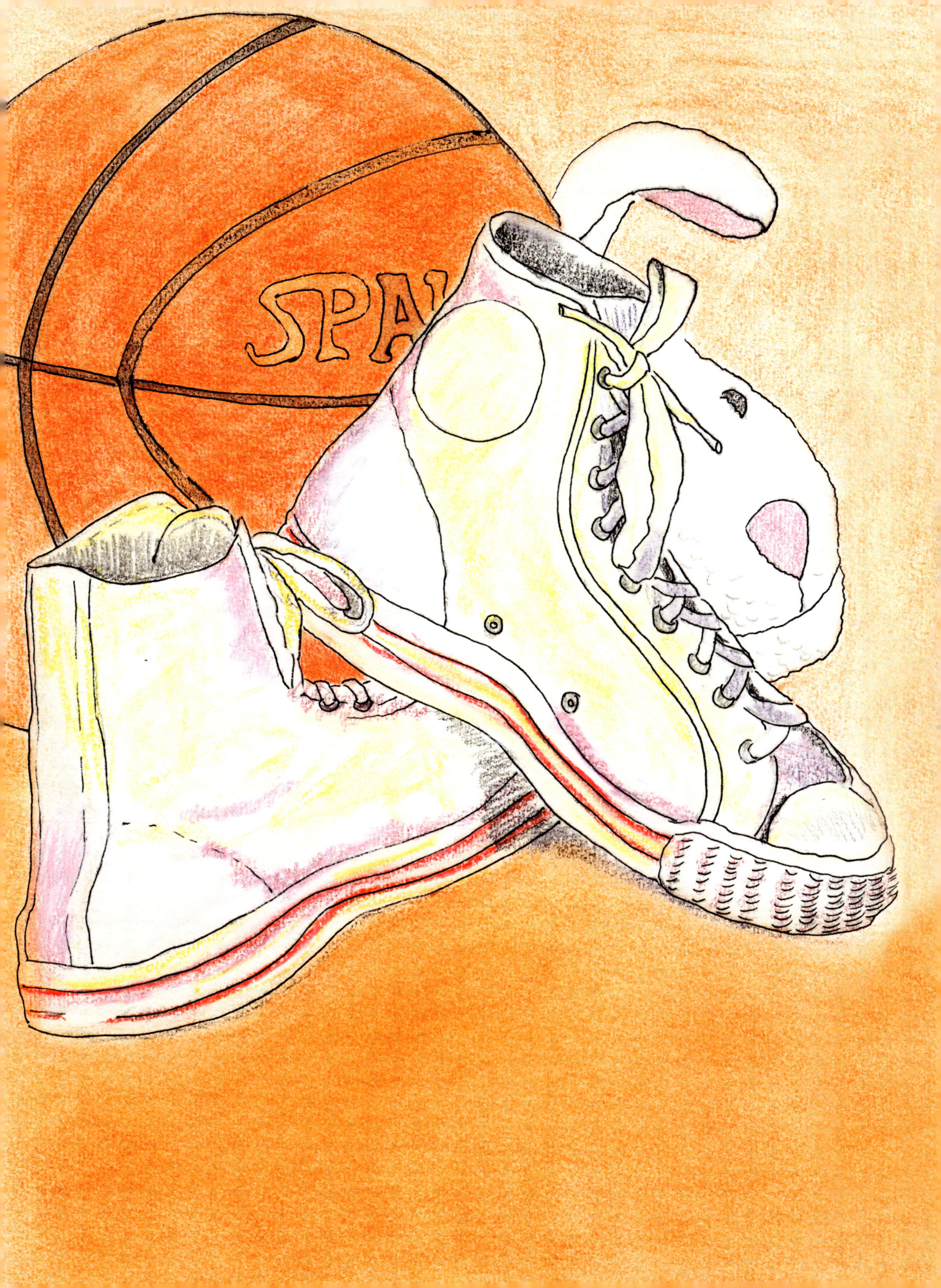
SPAL

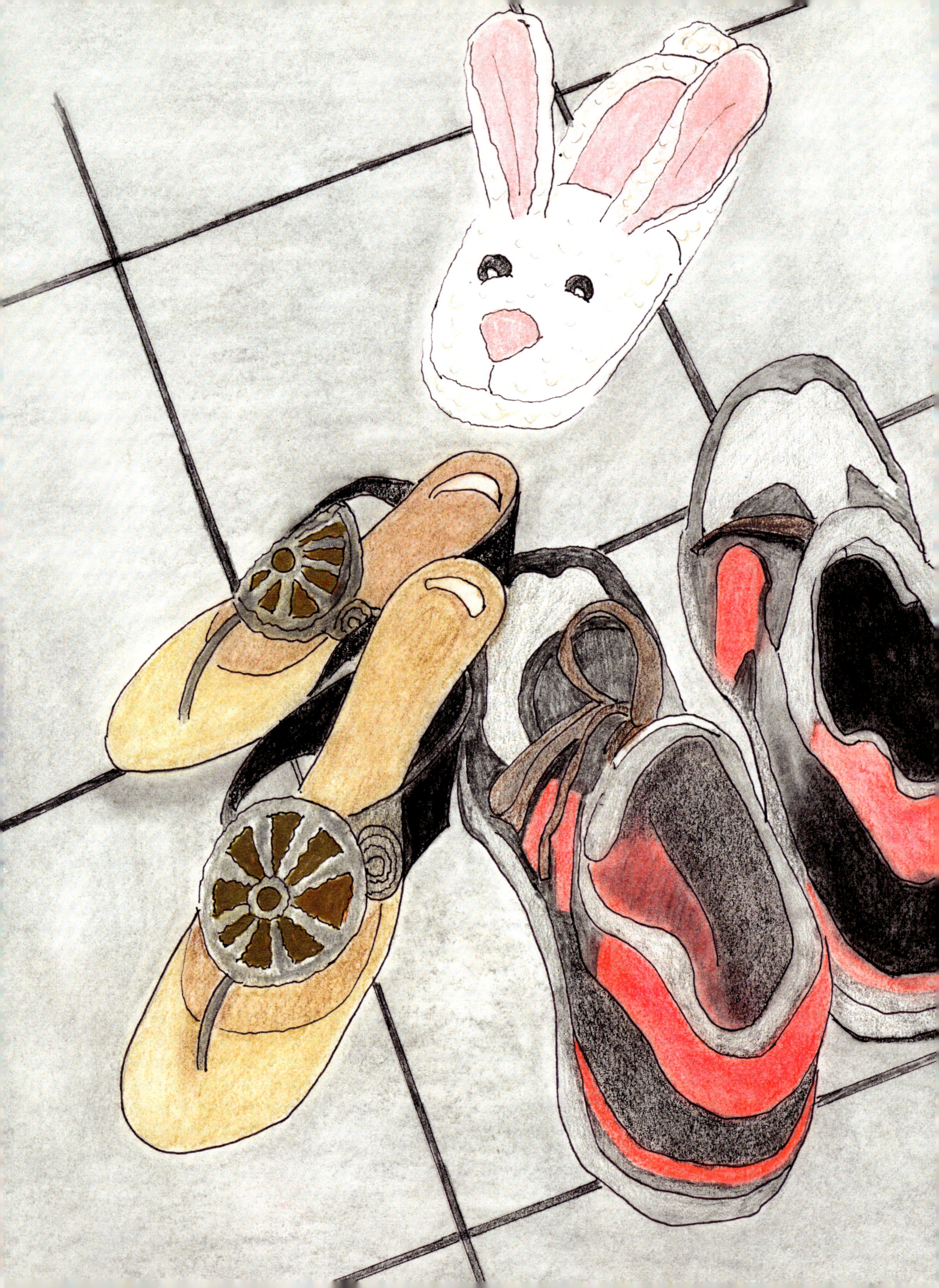

And then there were "new" friends who came one day.

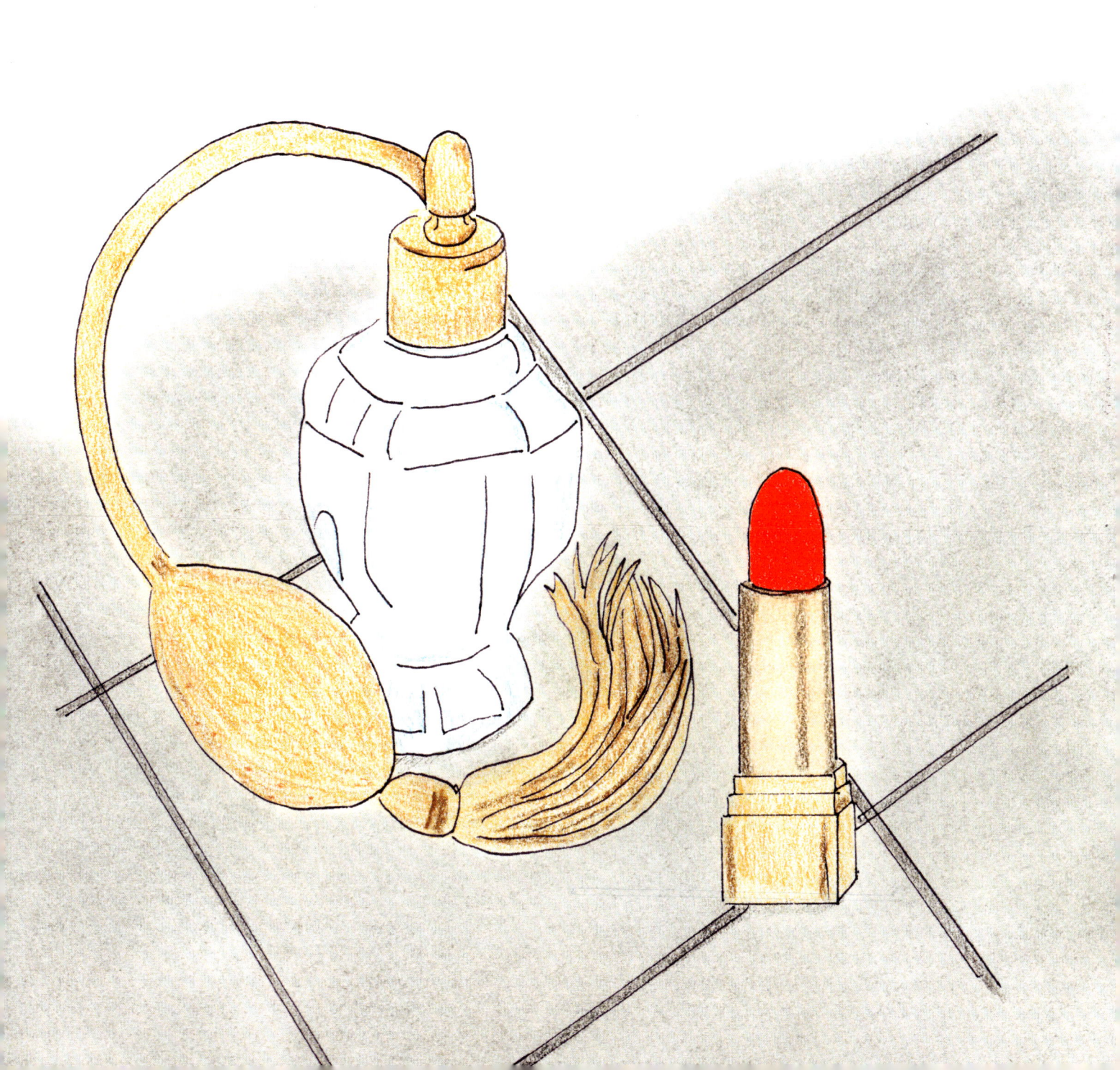

The friends did come,
by ones and by twos.

All friends were welcome
at the house full of shoes.

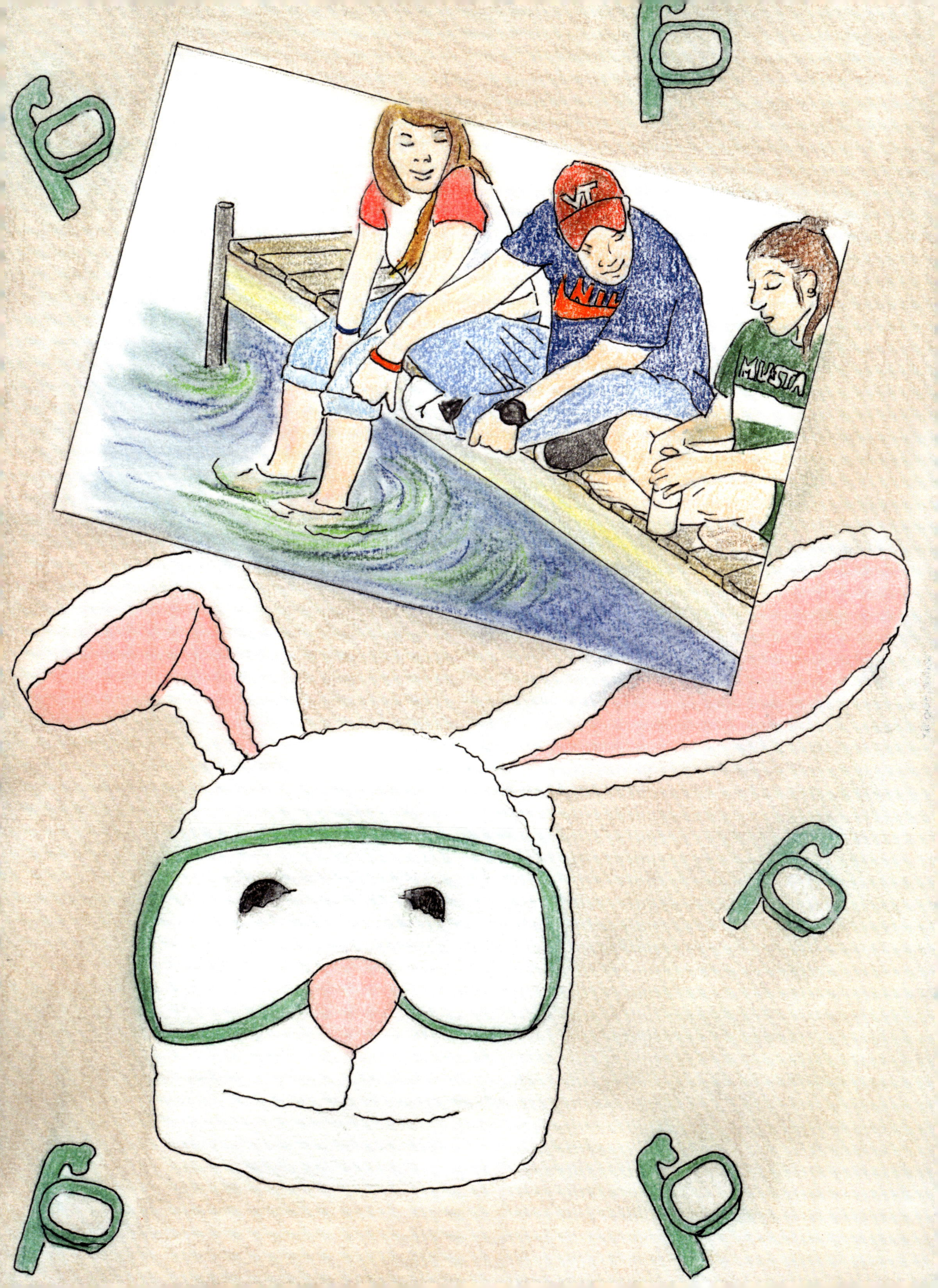

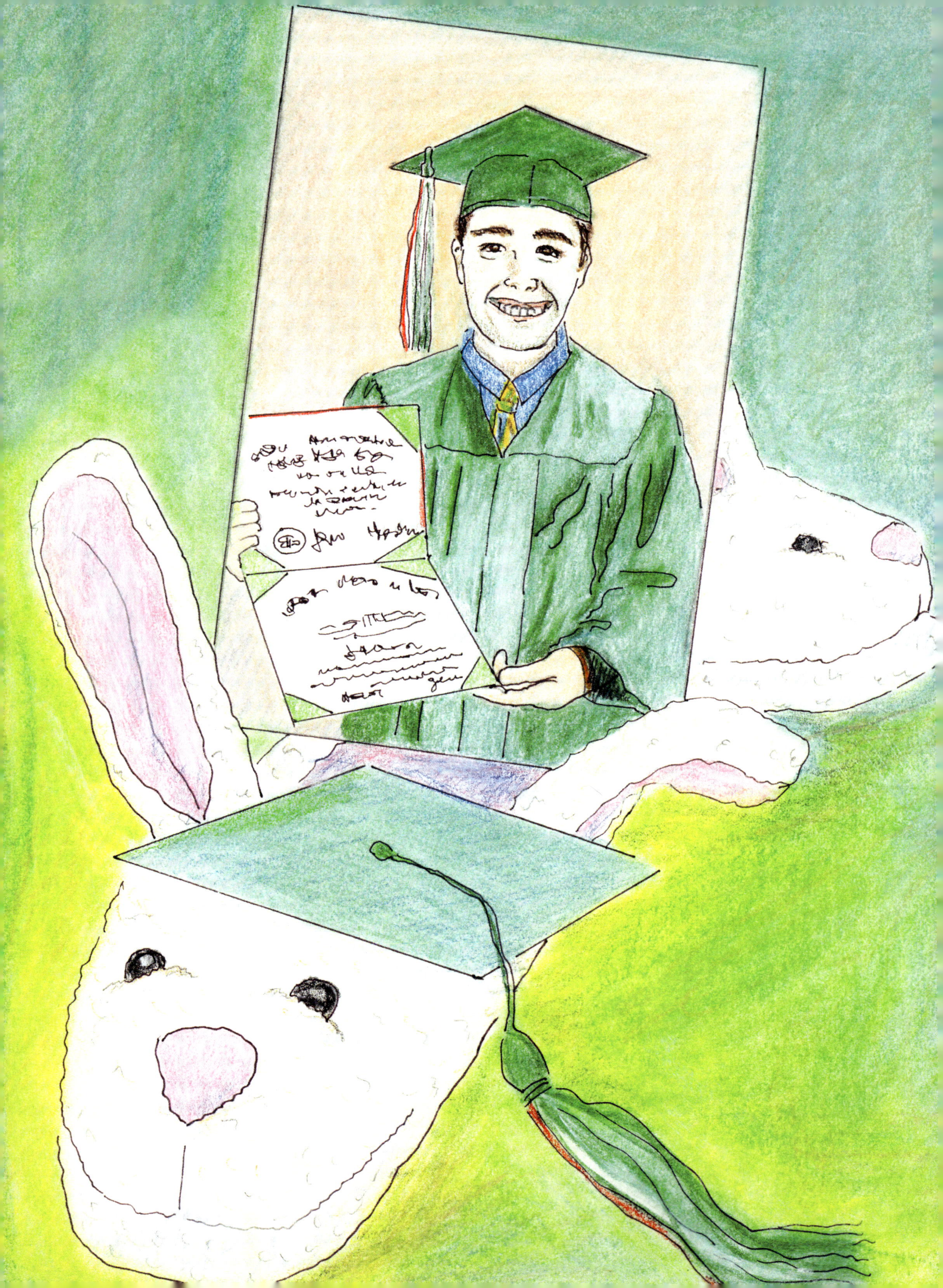

The brothers grew up,
as children will do.

And the house full of shoes went from many to few.

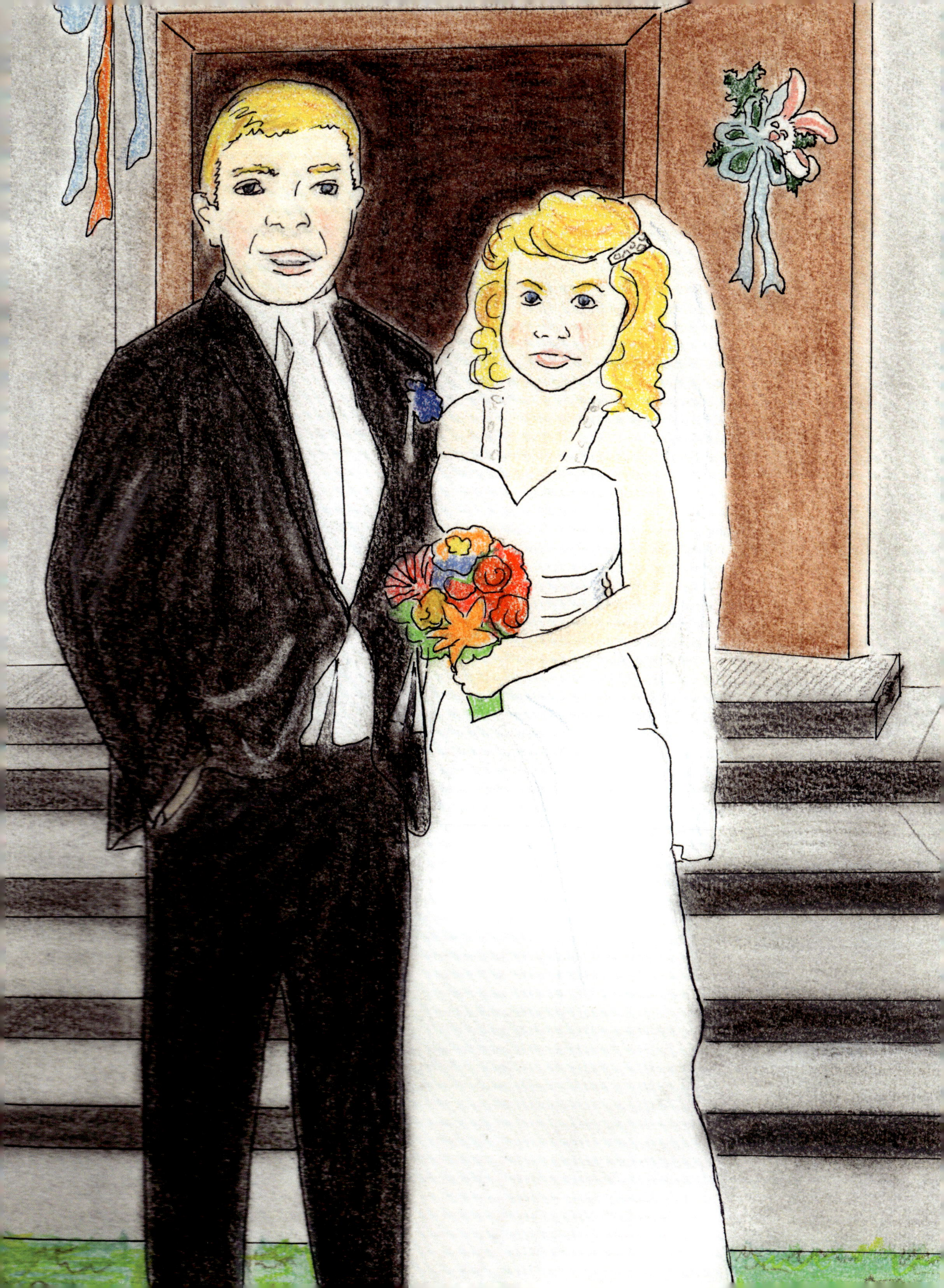

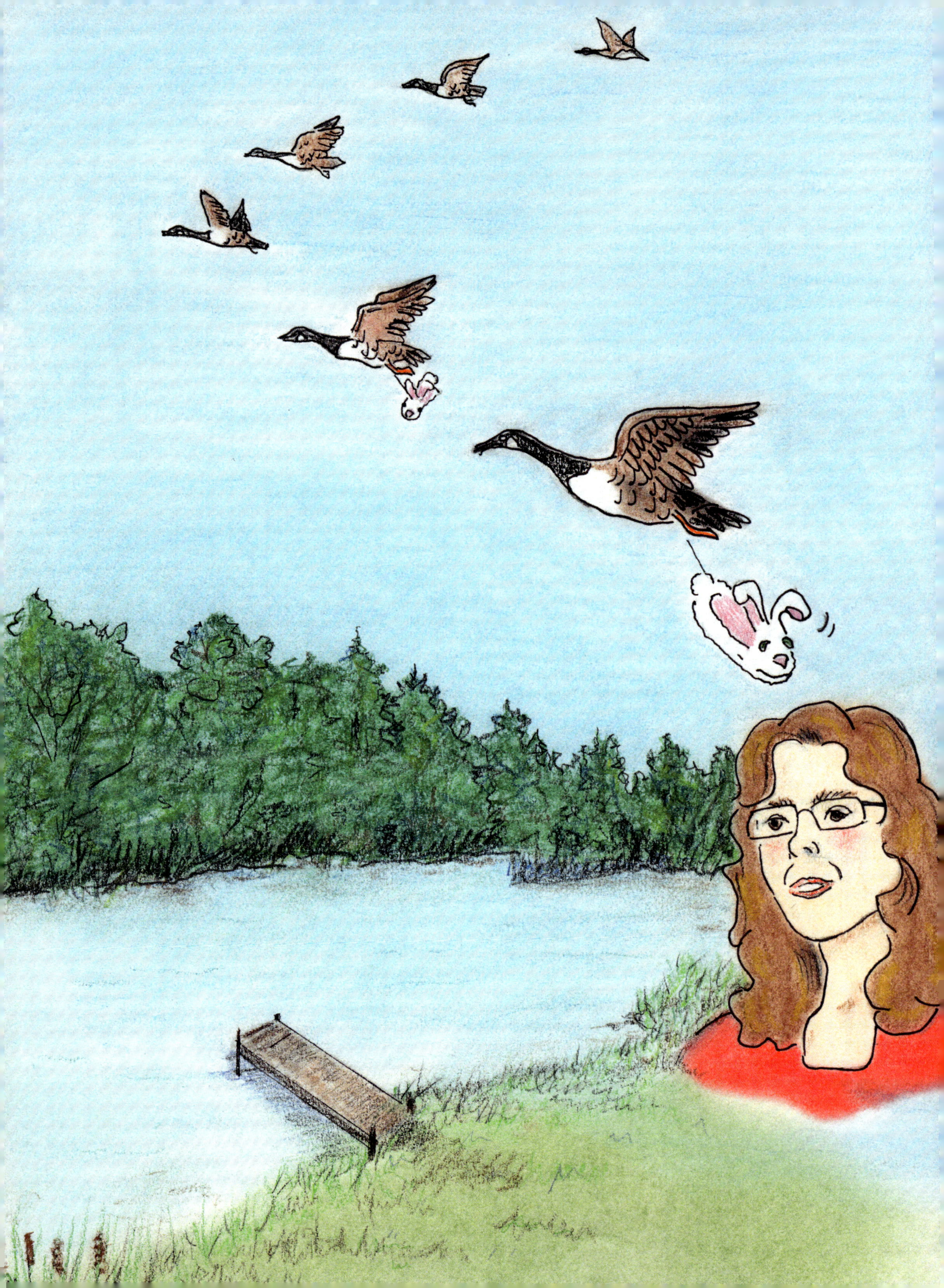

Strange thing to miss,
shoes of all things.

The shoes were now gone,
as if they took wing.

The house was so clean.
No clutter in sight.

Just what Mom wanted.
Now isn't that right?

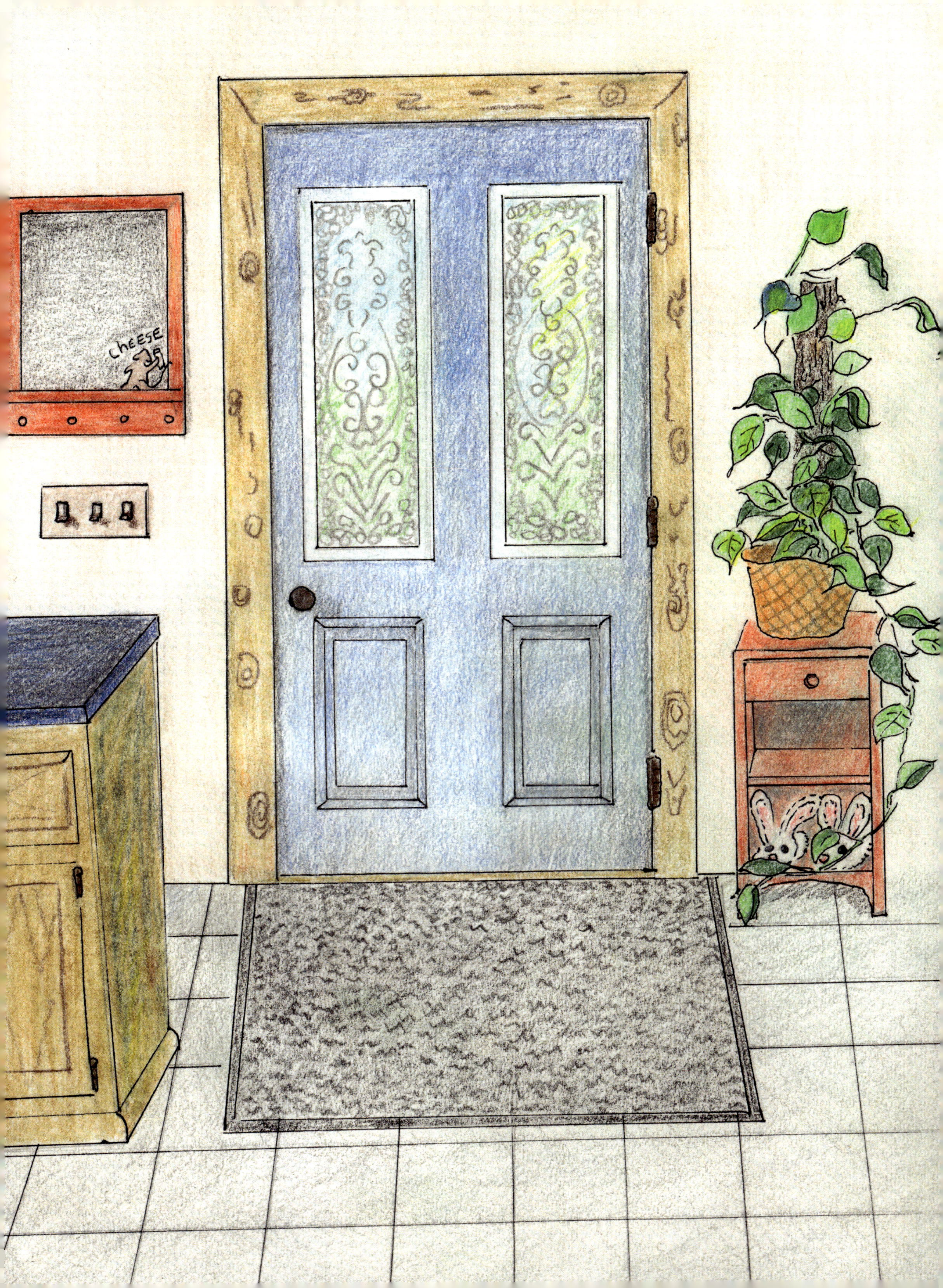
CHEESE

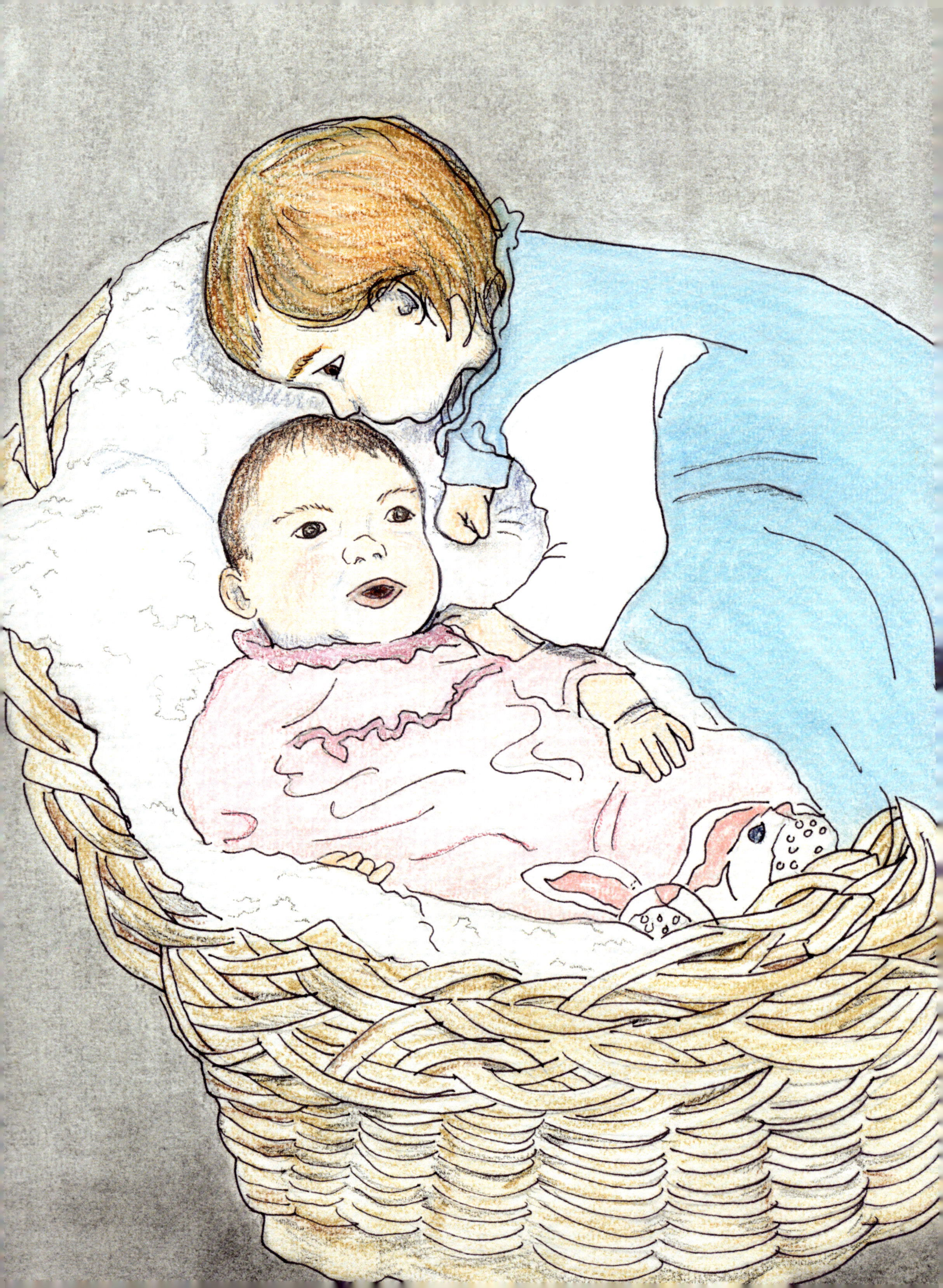

Time kept on marching,
and faster than fast,
there were new shoes to buy.

Grandparents at last!

When the kids came to visit with their shoes in a pile, Grandma would look at those shoes and just smile.

"Don't touch those shoes. Don't put them away."

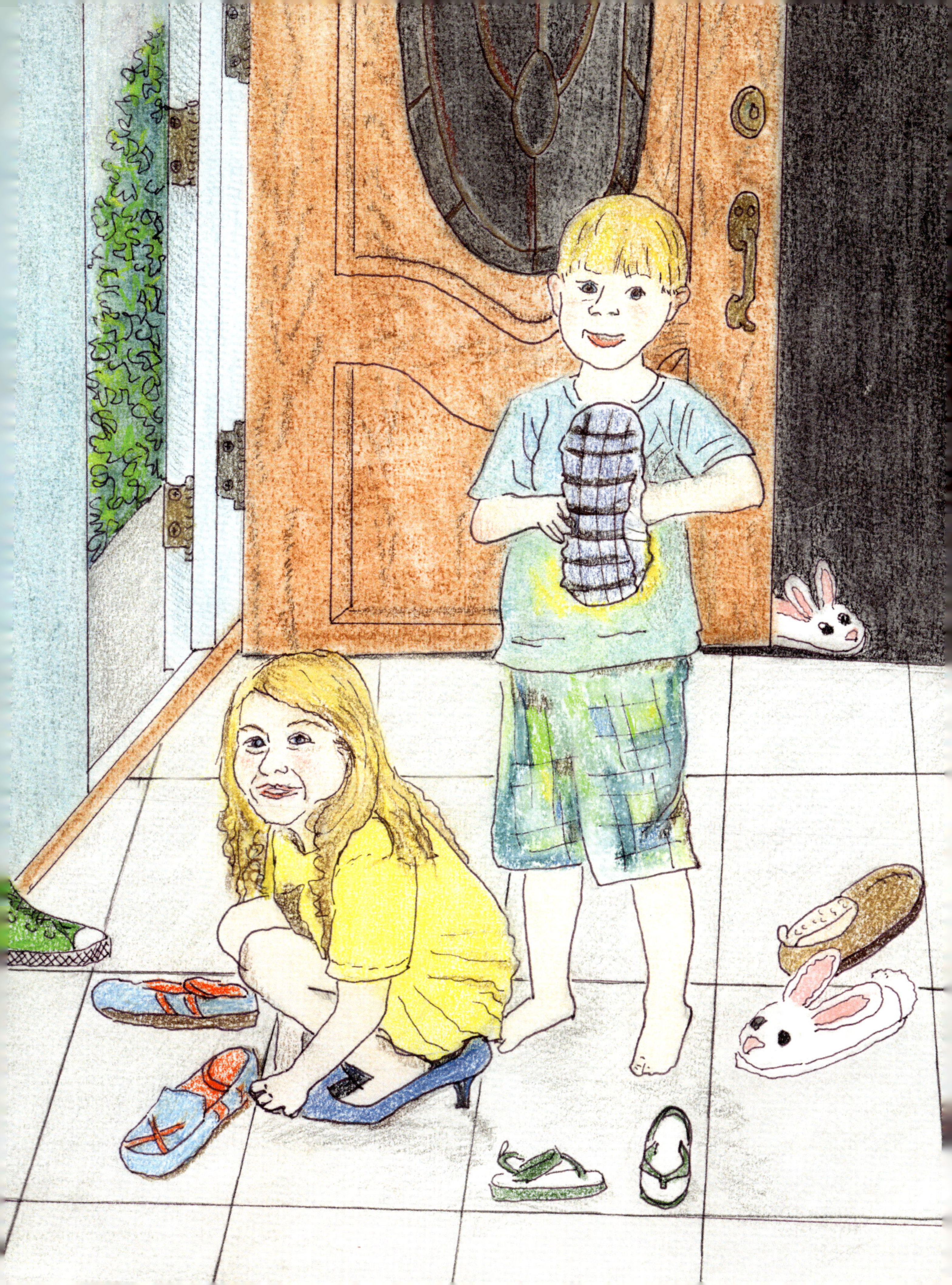

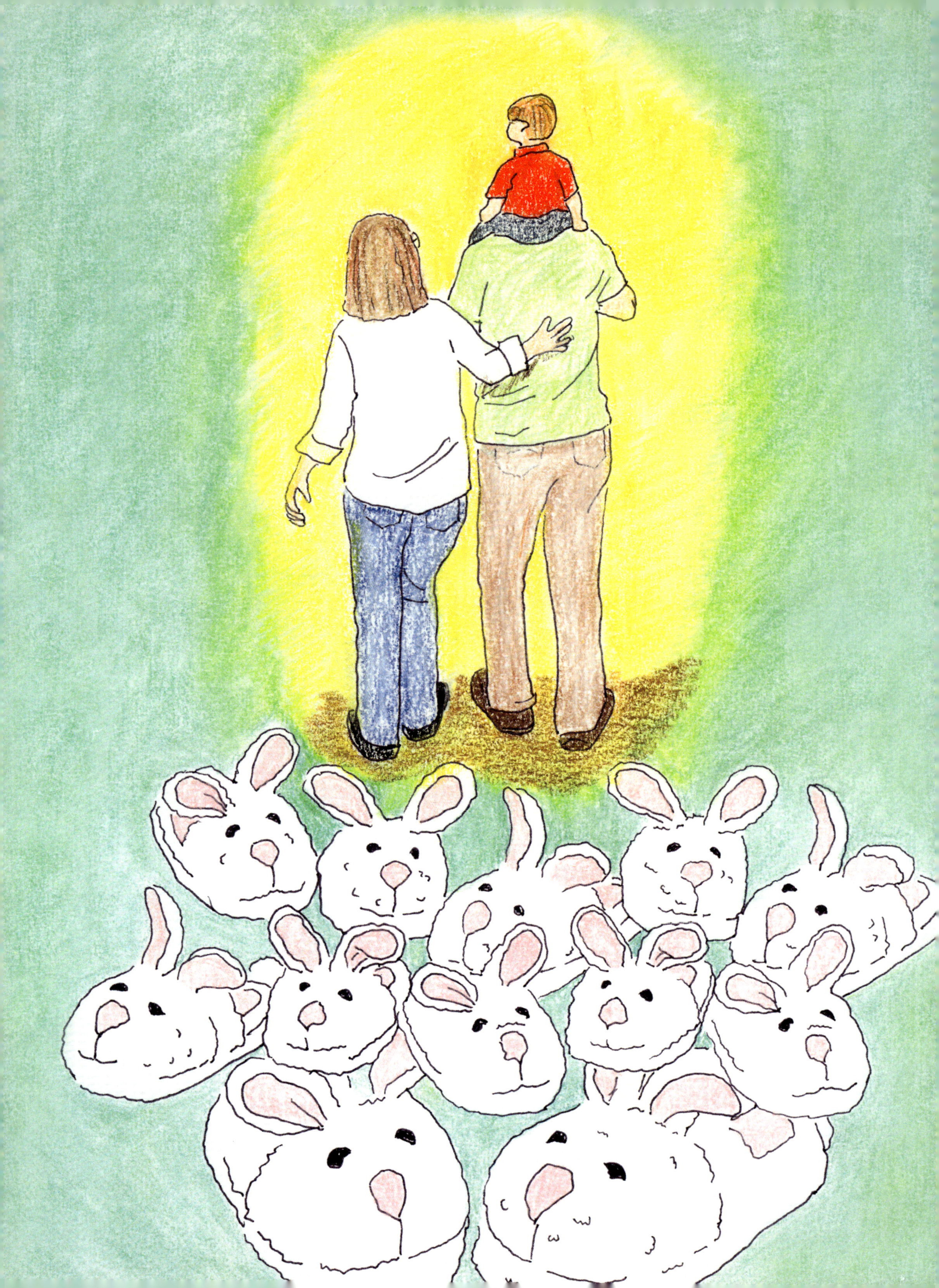

"I've missed all those shoes and I want them to stay."

To Jake and Chad.

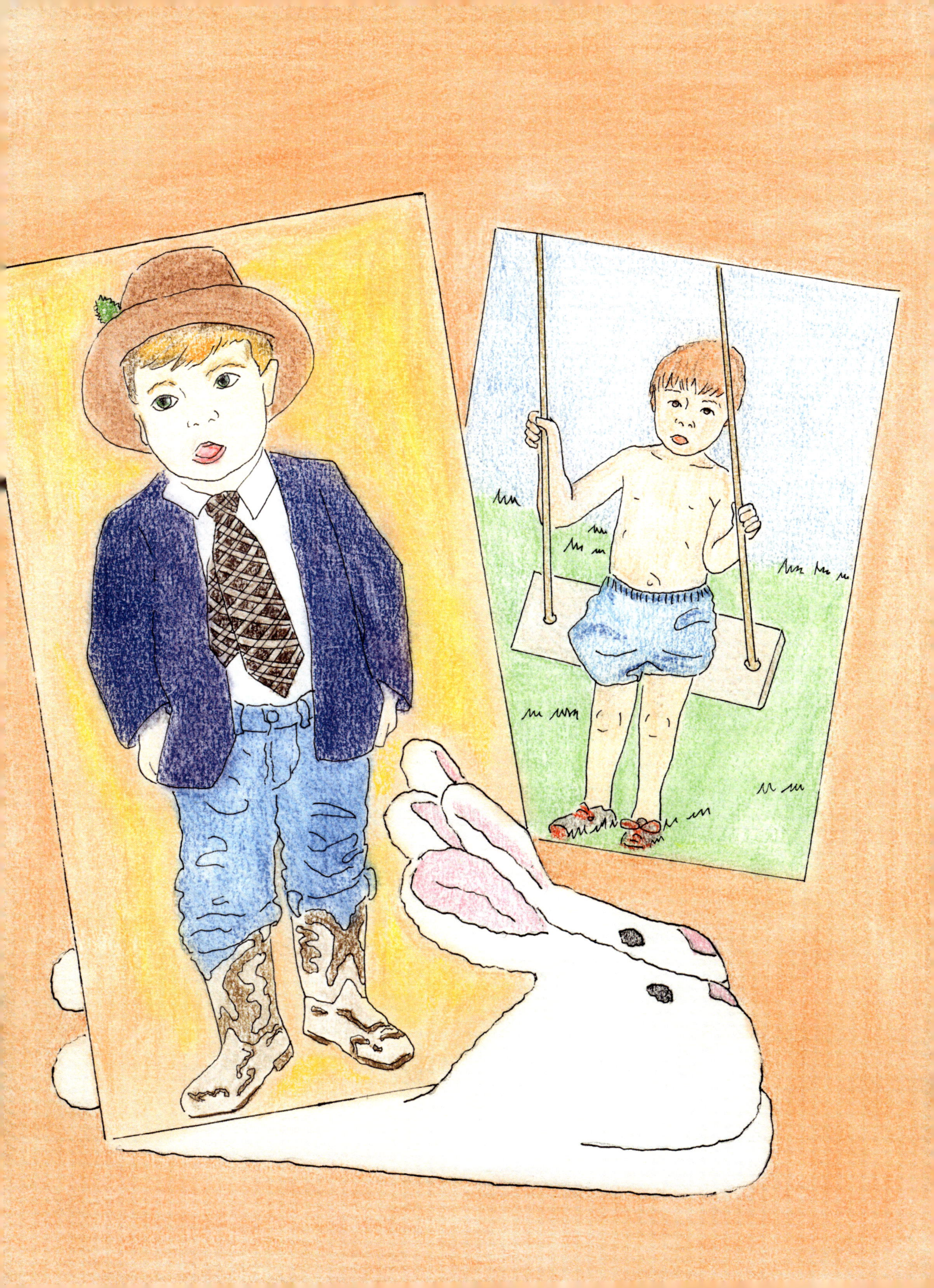

Other works by this author:

The Bear Song is a popular Boy/Girl Scout camp song. It is called an echo song because the leader sings the first line and waits while the echo repeats it. They then sing the chorus together.

The Bear Song is currently available on Amazon.com and Barnes & Noble online.

About the Author:

Kim Bedore Weinheimer was born in the small Adirondack town of Tupper Lake. She and her husband live outside of Syracuse, NY where she works at a hospital as a Medical Technologist.

"I wrote and illustrated this book as I became an empty nester. The book was written for my family initially – but then I could see that children, new parents and empty nesters could share in my experience. What I wanted to express was the joy I experienced in all the moments and phases of parenting. And even though we are now empty nesters, we stay busy with our own lives and look forward to great moments – and shoes – yet to come.

I hope you enjoy reading this book as much as I enjoyed making it.

P.S. - I have placed bunny slippers throughout the pages of this book. Think of it as a treasure hunt. How many can you find?"

Kim

A new adventure from Kim Weinheimer.
Coming soon...